BABY NATASHA
in
"Say Cheese!"

By Liza Alexander
Illustrated by Joe Ewers

A GOLDEN BOOK • NEW YORK

**Published by Golden Books Publishing Company, Inc., in cooperation
with Children's Television Workshop**

The Furry Arms

Elmo raced around the corner and spun through the revolving doors of the Furry Arms Hotel. "Wheee!" He spun all the way around again just for fun. "Whirli-doors!" sang Elmo. "Elmo loves whirli-doors!"

Elmo was on his way to play with Baby Natasha. The little monster lived at the Furry Arms with her parents, Ingrid and Humphrey, who worked there.

Ingrid and Humphrey were in the lobby.

"Hi!" said Elmo. "What's up?"

"We're off to the photo studio!" answered Ingrid. "Today Natasha is to have her picture taken. Would you like to come along?"

"Oh, yes!" said Elmo.

"Wonderful!" said Ingrid. "Do we have everything, Humphrey, dear?"

"Let's see," he answered. "There's Natasha's stroller and her diaper bag, her fire truck, her high chair, her parasol . . ."

"But Humphrey," interrupted Elmo.

"One minute," he said. "I must be sure we have everything. There's your pocketbook, dearest, my cap, the badminton rackets, Natasha's jacket, her inflatable swimming pool . . ."

"Ingrid! Humphrey!" insisted Elmo. "Where's Natasha?"

"Oh, my goodness!" said Ingrid. "She slipped our minds. How silly! Maybe she's with our bellhop, Benjamin. Will you go check, Humphrey, my sweet?"

"Certainly, my dear," he answered. "Come along, Elmo."

The two monsters rode the elevator up to the top floor. There was Baby Natasha helping Benny the Bunny deliver suitcases. "Da-da!" cooed Natasha.

Humphrey scooped Natasha up. "Cootchie-cootchie-coo!" he said. "And Benjamin, many thanks for watching the baby!"

"Anytime!" said Benny. "*Ciao!*"

Finally the monsters set off through the hotel lobby and into the revolving doors. "Whirli-doors!" sang Elmo. "Whirli-doors! Wheee!"

"Oh, fiddlesticks," said Ingrid. "We've forgotten Natasha's pacifier. I'm sure I left it at the reception desk."

"Elmo will get it!" volunteered Elmo. He whirled back through the doors, still carrying Natasha, and hurried across the floor.

Sherry Netherland, the owner of the hotel, was working at the desk.
"Have you seen Natasha's pacifier?" asked Elmo.

"I most certainly have, young fella," snapped Sherry Netherland. "It's
cluttering up the mail slots, along with lots of other baby things. Get it
all out of my life, please!"

"No problem!" said Elmo. He set Natasha down and went behind the
desk. In the mail slots he found the pacifier, a rattle, some baby shoes,
and some bath toys. He collected everything, and once again, he and
Natasha were off.

Finally the monsters arrived at the photo studio. They were only two hours late! Humphrey staggered under his huge pile of stuff. The photographer was waiting and ready to take the picture. Elmo set Natasha down to pose on the special fuzzy rug.

But Natasha would not stay still. Off she crawled, back toward her daddy. Ingrid plucked Natasha up and plunked her back down on the fuzzy rug.

Elmo thought that Natasha might stay put if he played with her. He
tried peekaboo and eensy weensy spider, but the baby wasn't the least bit
interested in either game. Off she crawled again, back toward her daddy.

Elmo chose the pacifier, teddy monster, and rattle from Humphrey's pile and offered them to Natasha. The little monster gurgled, but she shook her little head "no."

The photographer was beginning to get impatient. He sighed, folded his arms across his chest, and tapped his foot, *tappity-tap-tap*, on the floor.

This time Elmo brought the baby her bottle, books, and bath toys. She batted them away.

Ingrid tooted the horn. Natasha scrunched up her face and pressed her little paws over her ears.

Off Natasha crawled again, back toward her daddy. Again Ingrid plucked her up and plunked her back down on the fuzzy rug. And then Natasha began to cry. Soon she was screaming and howling and shaking her little fists and feet.

"That's it," said the photographer. "I've had enough. Why don't you bring your baby back when she's in a better mood?" He began to put his camera away.

"Please," Ingrid said, "this isn't like Natasha. Just a few more minutes . . ."
At that moment Humphrey had had enough, too. He dropped
everything he was holding, and it all went flying! A piece of Swiss cheese
landed right smack on Natasha's lap. She grabbed it, took a bite, and began
to chew. And then—just like that—she smiled a big baby smile. Natasha
was hungry! That had been the problem all along.

Click! The photographer snapped a picture.

"Say cheese!" said the photographer as he took another picture.
And that's just what Ingrid, Humphrey, Elmo, and Baby Natasha did!